About the Author

Michael's first book in the series is inspired by real world events and a giant lop-eared rabbit called Mojoe who had astonishingly human traits.

Coming soon, *Mojoe And The Ballerina*, *Mojoe And The Onion Seller* and *Mojoe And The Missing Case*.

A CIP catalogue record for this title is
available from the British Library.

ISBN: 978-1-83934-327-8

Bumblebee Books is an imprint of
Olympia Publishers.

First Published in 2022

Bumblebee Books
Tallis House
2 Tallis Street
London
EC4Y 0AB

Printed in Great Britain

www.olympiapublishers.com

To India
Enjoy Mojoe's first book and adventure
Michael

Michael Forteath

Mojoe the Super Rabbit

Bumblebee Books
London

When you glanced at Mojoe she was no ordinary doe,
she did things and went places no one could know.
Behind her black and white fluff and adorable nose,
were stories of valour and battling with foes.

Mojoe didn't know she was born with a gift,
until the day a large boulder she just started to lift.
And when the other rabbits used to skip, jump and hop,
Mojoe was practising her super karate chop.

The other rabbits looked at her from afar,
when she was doing skids and turns in her super-fast car.
When they were all having normal rabbit fun,
she was improving her aim with her super carrot gun.

She often wondered why she knew all this stuff,
and why she seemed so incredibly tough.
But it didn't take long for her to find out why,
she could chop, shoot, drive and even fly!

Near to the farm where she grew up and slept,
was a large barn where cows and sheep were kept.
One morning the farmer began to shout when he awakened,
all his prize animals had mysteriously been taken.

By who and for what reasons, nobody could guess,
time for the super-rabbit her powers to test.
Out from the back of the warren she darted,
no time to lose, the search for the animals had started.

Which one of her super skills should she try,
to drive, fight or shoot or even to fly?
Yes, that was the one, and she rose in the sky
up, up over clouds as the landscape whizzed by.

From high in the sky, where she had risen,
she decided to use her super-rabbit vision.
Way off in the distance she saw animals to the left,
with a man at the front clearly involved in the theft!

So on she flew to rescue the group,
at speed, lower and lower she expertly swooped.
She decided the best way for the stealing to stop,
was to knock out the thief with her very best chop!

'Who do you think you are?' she said.
'These animals are not yours!
I may be a rabbit but I will return them for sure!'
'You can't stop me,' said the thief, 'you don't know how!'
Then she flipped in the air and with one chop – kerpow!

Back to the farm the animals she led,
all the way home until they were safe in their shed.
She was back in the warren before anybody worked out,
how they had returned and who gave the thief a clout.

'That I have these powers needs to stay secret,
with all I can do it's the best way to keep it.
So I'll hide my powers for as long as I can…'
But out of the darkness a little voice rang!

'Hi, I'm Katie,' said a small brown guinea pig,
'that was quite a thing that you just did.
A rabbit that can fly, that's quite a show,
but fear not, I can keep your secret you know.'

'It was amazing indeed, but I also won't tell,'
said a voice from deep within a tortoise shell.
Out popped a head. 'I'm George you see.'
And Mojoe's super team went from one to three!